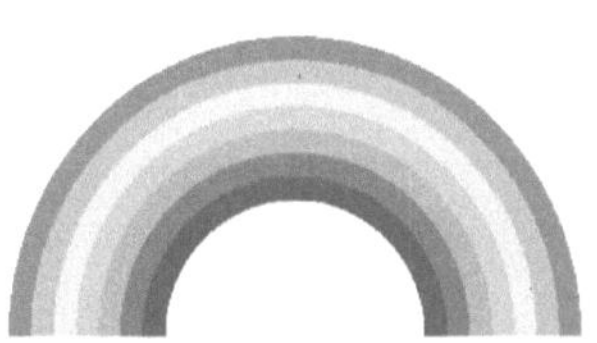

THE RAINBOW ROOM

THE RAINBOW ROOM

a short story

by Claire Ishi Ayetoro

www.ishiayetoro.com

www.ishiayetoro.com

in pursuit of the dream

white.

White is for the way you
WHISPERED to me…

A man stirs. In a bed, a cot. In a room. A white room. The air is still and stale.

"Ugh my head." He reaches a hand to his forehead and rubs his eyebrows. His head throbs with intense pain, as if his blood vessels would burst from the pressure of his beating heart; too much to drink last night. He had been to a party, a business gala. That is the last thing he remembered.

He sits up and looks around the room. This place is unfamiliar. It's got four walls; that's normal, but what's within those four walls is an arrangement that he has not yet witnessed until now.

The room is wide open. A rectangle. About 50 feet long and 20 feet wide. There is a single cot in the middle of the floor and a large light on the ceiling above the cot, your normal, everyday white light. Looking to the north wall, he sees a large monitor screen. The south wall contains what looks like a shut window with a large protruding lip underneath. The west wall contains nothing. It is empty. The east wall contains a door. It is open.

An open door.

*He decides to get up from the cot and
exit this room, try to find someone
who can give him some answers. He
approaches the door, but before he can
get to the opening, it slides down
sealed and shut.*

"Bam!"

He stops mid stride. Perfect. Now he's trapped. Like a mouse in a maze. Except there is nothing of a maze here. Only an open room.

The light above turns to a soft blue, and something like elevator music begins to play.

"Hello? Is anyone there?"

The man raises his voice to get someone's attention. He knew there was someone there, and he had to begin his questioning. Someone had to be monitoring him.

"Hello!" he says louder, more adamantly.

Still no answer.

Where the hell am I?

The reality was beginning to sink in that wherever he was, his experience wouldn't be comparable to being at a Ritz Carlton hotel having dinner with colleagues. Which, ironically, led him to this place.

*He decided to walk around the room to
see if there was any other possible way
of escape.*

He walked to the door and pressed around its perimeter. Maybe there was a secret button that would recess and allow the door to open. No such luck.

He walked over to the shut window.
There wasn't even so much as a gap to
slide his fingers underneath.

He walked back to the cot and sat down. A feeling of defeat eased over his features.

The monitor screen comes on, and a message flashes across it.

"NO BAD DEED GOES UNPUNISHED."

This is what the screen read.

He looks up and reads it silently.

Now what is that supposed to mean?

He thought. That could mean anything. It was a fact that screwing people over was part of his job. He had crossed more people than he could put fingers to.

His name is

Jack Taylor.

blue.

Blue is for the way you BLEW my mind...

The elevator music was still playing over the speaker. It was getting rather annoying, but suddenly, it struck a chord within him.

It reminded him of a past time. He remembered now. This was the song that played on his wedding day, at the first dance. "I Only Have Eyes for You." Yes, that was why it was so annoying.

The monitor screen comes on again, and another message flashes across it.

"I COME IN THE MORNING, I COME AT NOONDAY, I COME AT NIGHT. WHEN I COME, I AWAKEN YOU TO THE REST OF YOUR LIFE."

Is this some kind of joke?

Not a joke. That is more in the form of...a riddle. Yes, that was what it was he decided.

Then, another message.

"YOU HAVE 35 MINUTES."

The number "35" flashes across the screen.

The shut window opens. There is an item there. He walks over to the window and examines it. A pail. An empty pail. He picks up the pail and suddenly, he hears three bells ascending in a pleasant tone.

He looks toward the screen and a green "O" has appeared. He sets the pail down. At that, he hears an ominous brassy tone and a red "X" appears on the screen. Bad move. He picks the pail up again and brings it to the cot with him.

He sets the pail aside.

*Think. Think. Think. I'm in a room.
With a pail and a riddle. I have
thirty-five minutes to do whatever it
is I need to do. But I don't know what
that is exactly.*

"What the fuck do you want me to do!?"

He shouts in frustration.

*The riddle flashes on the screen
again.*

*"I COME IN THE MORNING, I
COME AT NOONDAY, I COME
AT NIGHT. WHEN I COME, I
AWAKEN YOU TO THE REST OF
YOUR LIFE."*

My god.

"An orgasm."

He attempts to answer the riddle without much thought. Just to test the waters.

He immediately hears the brassy tone, but this time, two red "X's" show up on the monitor.

Okay, that's two strikes. Maybe try a little harder.

"A dog?"

He tries again. The brassy sound projects from the speakers and three red "X's" appear on the monitor.

The monitor flickers and switches to a video feed. He sees his most prized possession. His 2014 Lamborghini Veneno Roadster. Four men in all black attire from head to toe surrounded it, each with a bat in his possession.

His heart fell into his stomach. Beads of sweat began to break out on his forehead, and his skin turned cold. As he watched, the men began to assault and batter his Lamborghini.

Each man took a side. They beat in the windows. They beat in the doors. One lifted the front hood and began cutting hoses and removing parts from the hood assembly.

Jack looked on in agony. He screamed in anguish as he watched the dreadful act. His body pained as if he was being beaten himself. He pulled at his brown hair as he looked on with his blue eyes. His aged 49 body of medium build sunk to the blue lit floor.

The music once playing smoothly now repeated, stuck on the phrase "I only have eyes... I only have eyes... I only have eyes..."

The scene switched to a junk yard where his beaten Lamborghini was parked. A large machine lifted the vehicle into a rectangular capsule. The roof of the capsule began to descend onto the car, crushing it to nothingness. The screen then went blank.

Jack, curled up on the floor, had a new perspective. He realized that his predicament was a serious one, and whoever had him under their control meant business.

The screen flashed "30." The light turned a bright green. He heard a loud screeching sound and noticed that the east and west walls closed in a measure.

green.

Green is for the GIFTS you gave
me...

The music stops. In its place, the green light begins to flicker incessantly. Jack felt he may have a seizure with the lights going in and out as they were.

A message flashes on the screen.

"WHAT'S DONE IN THE DARK
MUST COME TO LIGHT."

Then, the riddle once again.

*"I COME IN THE MORNING, I
COME AT NOONDAY, I COME
AT NIGHT. WHEN I COME, I
AWAKEN YOU TO THE REST OF
YOUR LIFE."*

*He gets up off the floor. Time to get
serious.*

He doesn't immediately spew an answer to the riddle this time. He now knows that things can go horribly wrong. He loved his cars, and that Lamborghini had cost him millions. He thought back to his collection at his home. Had any more been touched? Had any more been violated as this one was?

"Let me out of here!"

He shouted.

"When I get out of here, you will have hell to pay! Don't think for one second that I won't find out who you are, because I will!"

He is angry. Fuming. Who dares to mess with him in this way? Do they not know who he is? He takes a hand through his brown hair, and in his anger, he kicks the pail. It sails across the room and clangs on the floor before rolling around and coming to a stop.

*At this, he hears the ascending bells
and three "O's" flash up on the screen.
What is this supposed to mean?*

The shut window opens again. Another item. He walks over to the counter to see what has been delivered. It is... a pile of earthworms. Gross.

What am I supposed to do with these?

He walks over to the pail, picks it up, and takes it to the counter where he scoops the worms inside.

*He takes the pail and sits on the cot.
He takes both of his big, hard hands
and rubs his face with them.*

How did he end up here? What kind of wrong turn did he make?

His face was full of stubble. He wished for a nice shave, a nice warm shower, and something to eat. Those things would make him feel a lot better.

The screen flicked on again. This time, it played another video. Jack watched intently, not knowing what to expect.

To his surprise, it was a rather pleasant show. It was an old video. A video of him and his family. His wife Olivia and his son Jack Jr. They were in the backyard of their home. It was summer and they had the grill going. Those were good times. Times before he made it big, and before his marriage went sour.

He had been married for 35 years, and now, it was barely hanging on by a thread. Admittedly, his work had taken over his life, but it was something he was proud of. How many people could say they started their own tech company from the ground up? He had fought his way to the top, and no one was going to take that away from him.

After thinking for some time, he decided to try another answer to the riddle.

"Ambition." He answered.

This was incorrect. He heard the brassy sound, and a red "X" appeared on the monitor.

He dropped his head.

What am I going to do?

He needed to figure something out. If he didn't, he may soon suffer a similar fate as his Lamborghini.

The monitor flashes "25." The light turns yellow. The east and west walls move in closer.

yellow.

*Yellow is for the way I YIELDED
my soul...*

Thank god the blinking lights had stopped. He didn't know how much more of that he could take—as if he had a choice.

As he sits on the cot, he swats a fly from his nose. He swats another from buzzing around his ear.

What the...

*He looks around the room. There are
flies everywhere.*

First the music, then the blinking lights, now the flies? They must have been introduced through a vent overhead. Whoever it was had it in for him. He absolutely hated flies. They reminded him of filth and lowliness. Two things he felt could never characterize him. But what did it matter? If he didn't figure out what was going on in the next 25 minutes, he thought he would be fly food. Regardless of if he guessed the riddle wrong or not, there were going to be consequences. In the next 25 minutes, he might be as flat as the fly he just smashed beneath his foot.

Should he focus on the items? Or should he focus on the riddle? Nothing seemed to make any sense. When he kicked the pail, that seemed to be a good thing. Because the green "O's" appeared and the pleasant sound and the new item: worms. He decided to focus on the worms.

He picked up the pail. The worms were slimy. They moved, sliding against each other in the pail. Disgusting. There were a good many of them. He wondered how many there were, so he began to count them all.

*One by one, he took each worm out of
the bucket and proceeded to count them
all. 1..2...3...9...16....24...*

"35... 35 worms!"

He shouted.

Three green "O's" appear on the screen with the audible of three ascending bells.

He breathed a sigh of relief. At least he did something right. Maybe if he had enough positive interactions with the items, he would find his way out of there soon.

Another item arrives at the window.

He moves through the cloud of flies to
get to the counter and inspect the new
item.

Flowers.

So far, he had collected a pail, 35 worms, and some flowers. Great.

*He took the flowers and put them in
the pail along with the worms.*

The screen flashes "20." The light turns orange. The room closes in even more.

orange.

Orange is for the OPENNESS of my heart…

Jack began to feel the cool of water on his skin. Rain? No.

Sprinklers.

Sprinklers from the ceiling drizzled water down to the ground below. Soon, he would be drenched in water.

The length of the room had reduced from about 50 feet to approximately 10 feet.

He began to go stir crazy. He wondered what more could be done to torture him. What more did this sick person have in mind?

A message flashes across the monitor.

*"WHAT YOU'VE DONE CAN'T
BE WASHED AWAY."*

Jack was nearing his breaking point.

"I'm sorry! I'm sorry okay! Whatever I did... All the things I've done. I can't take them back, but I'm sorry... I... I don't know what I can do to make up for it..."

Jack sits on the cot in defeat.

Was he really a bad person? What kind of question was that? Of course it was true. Deep down he knew it, no matter what excuse he tried to make for himself. He was beginning to feel a true remorse for his actions. He didn't have any true friends. Everyone kept a safe distance. They knew that when it came to his success, he would spare no one and nothing to get what he wanted.

*With his time dwindling, he decided
to guess at the riddle again.*

"Money?" Wrong. Two "X's."

Careful. Think harder. Maybe he needed to change his frame of thought. Come in from a different angle. One more "X" and who knows what would come up on that screen.

"Purpose." Wrong again. "Dammit!"

"XXX" flashes on the screen. Next a video pops up on the screen.

A woman appears with a noose around her neck. Her hands and feet are bound, and she weeps in desperation.

*His heart rises into his throat, and he
swallows hard. A nervous heat begins
to emanate from his body.*

"Carmen..." he whispers.

A message appears on the screen.

"DID YOU SLEEP WITH HER?"

Jack pauses. He does not answer.

Again, the screen flashes.

"DID YOU SLEEP WITH HER?"

Jack is still silent. He does not know how to answer. To answer in the affirmative, would be to incriminate himself. And who in the hell knew about his and Carmen's relationship? He was sure they were careful not to be discovered. Carmen was a colleague turned lover. She had been the reason he remained sane within his own marriage. He didn't want her caught up in this along with him.

"Who are you!?" He shouted.

On the screen, the noose around Carmen's neck began to lift. Carmen began to rise in the air, she struggled as the weight of her body dangled from the rope. She could not scream; she could not make a sound. Only her body's writhing could speak of her fear.

"Yes! Yes, okay? I... I slept with her..."

Suddenly, the rope was cut and Carmen's body fell to the ground. The screen cut to black.

Jack slipped from the cot onto the wet floor his face an entire wrinkle. He was sobbing, heaving. Crying.

"15" flashes on the screen. The light turns red. The walls close in a measure more.

red.

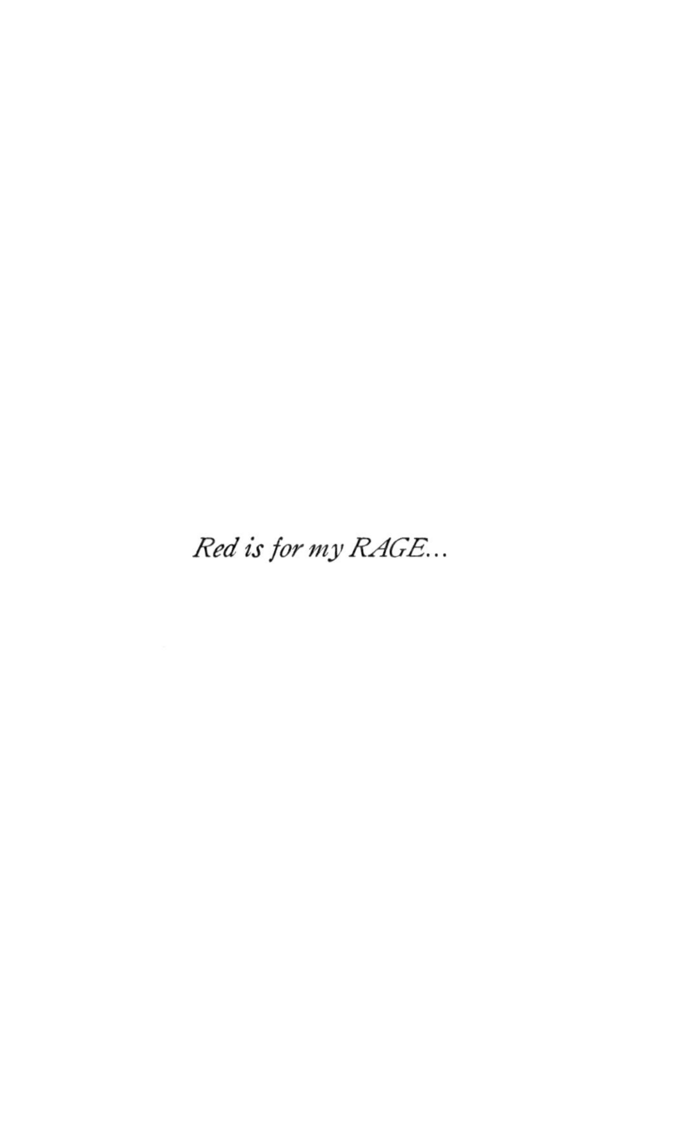

Red is for my RAGE…

The sprinklers shut off.

A rush of air is heard coming from above. Frigid air begins to blow into the small space.

Jack cries harder.

The riddle appears on the screen once more.

"I COME IN THE MORNING, I COME AT NOONDAY, I COME AT NIGHT. WHEN I COME, I AWAKEN YOU TO THE REST OF YOUR LIFE."

"I don't know!" shouts Jack.

"X"

"Truth!?"

"XX"

Jack curls up on the wet cot. Crying and cold. He takes a moment to wallow in his own self-pity.

I'm a dead man.

He dared not give another answer unless he was sure it was his best.

He must think harder. Maybe not harder, smarter. He must think smarter. Those items had to be clues to the riddle's answer. They were the only thing that gave him positive responses from the monitor.

What did the items have to do with this?

*He thought. When he kicked the pail,
somehow that was a clue. But why?
Did it have something to do with his
anger? Or was it the physical act of
kicking the pail? Did it have some type
of significance?*

Kick the pail. Kicking the pail. Pail?
Or... Bucket? Kicking the bucket...
Kick the bucket.

Ah... That would make sense. To "kick the bucket" is a common phrase. A euphemism for... death. What about the worms though? He had counted them. Counting worms? Did that have something to do with death as well? Then, there were the flowers. What kind of flowers were those? After some thought, he guessed that they may have been daisies.

He goes over the riddle in his mind. The rest of your life. Maybe, instead of being the remainder of life, this meant the best sleep of life. The "Big Sleep." He wasn't positive, but he figured his next guess was as good as it was going to get.

"Death. The answer is death."

The light turns white, and the walls begin to lengthen to their original position.

rainbow.

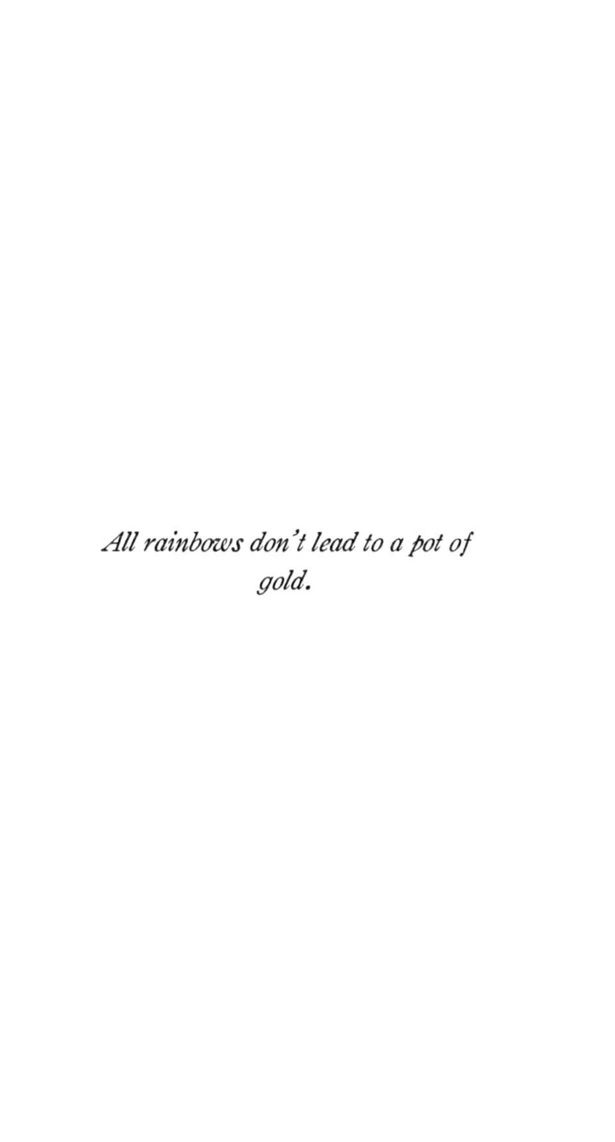

All rainbows don't lead to a pot of gold.

Jack watched as the walls receded.

It seemed as if everything was over.
He looked across the wet, fly-ridden
room.

He looked to the monitor. There was nothing. No words. No video. But he was still there. That meant that all was not over.

*Suddenly and simultaneously, the
door opened and the window opened.*

He walked to the window to see what it was. It was a plate of food. It smelled gorgeous. The presentation included steak, asparagus, mashed potatoes, and on the side, a glass of red wine. There was also a note.

Jack reads the note. He turns pale.

He sprints for the open door, but before he gets to the door, it shuts...again.

Jack continues to run toward the door and proceeds to beat at it with his fists and kick it with his heels. He now knew that there was no escape.

*He walked back over to the plate of food
and glass of wine. He picked them up
and brought them over to the cot. He
put the glass of wine on the floor next
to the cot and sat the plate at the head
of the bed. He began to eat.*

He takes a bite of the mashed potatoes. They are flaky and buttery. His favorite kind.

*He takes a bite of the asparagus. It
has the perfect crunch, just how he
likes it.*

*He takes a bite of the steak. It is juicy
and tender. Perfect.*

He drinks a sip of wine. Underneath the sweet taste of red grapes, it is bitter. Just what he was waiting for. It did not take long for the wine to have its effect, and Jack soon fell face forward into his plate of food.

*The note read: "Hell hath no fury like
a woman scorned. – Your Wife"*

***

THE

END

ALSO BY

CLAIRE ISHI AYETORO

I HEAR THE BLACK RAVEN: A PETITE MEMOIR

A LEAF FOR BONGANI: A NOVELETTE